SOPHIE'S TROPHY

Susan Middleton Elya

illustrated by Viviana Carofoli

G. P. PUTNAM'S SONS

To Susan Kochan, a great editor who knows
toads really do speak Spanish.

—S.M.E.

For April.

—V.G.

G. P.
PUTNAM'S SONS
A division of Penguin Young
Readers Group. Published by The
Penguin Group. Penguin Group (USA) Inc.,
375 Hudson Street, New York, NY 10014, U.S.A.
Penguin Group (Canada), 90 Eglinton Avenue East,
Suite 700, Toronto, Ontario, Canada M4P 2Y3 (a division of
Pearson Penguin Canada Inc.). Penguin Books Ltd, 80 Strand,
London WC2R 0RL, England. Penguin Ireland, 25 St. Stephen's
Green, Dublin 2, Ireland (a division of Penguin Books Ltd.). Penguin
Group (Australia), 250 Camberwell Road, Camberwell, Victoria 3124,
Australia (a division of Pearson Australia Group Pty Ltd). Penguin Books
India Pvt Ltd, 11 Community Centre, Panchsheel Park, New Delhi - 110 017, India.
Penguin Group (NZ), Cnr Airborne and Rosedale Roads, Albany, Auckland 1310, New
Zealand (a division of Pearson New Zealand Ltd). Penguin Books (South Africa) (Pty)
Ltd, 24 Sturdee Avenue, Rosebank, Johannesburg 2196, South Africa. Penguin Books Ltd,
Registered Offices: 80 Strand, London WC2R 0RL, England.

Manufactured in China by South China Printing Co. Ltd. Design by Gina DiMassi. The art was done in acrylics.
Text set in Font Soup Catalan Boiled. Library of Congress Cataloging-in-Publication Data Elya, Susan Middleton,
1955– Sophie's trophy / Susan Middleton Elya ; illustrated by Viviana Garofoli. p. cm. Summary: Sophie the toad
wishes she were as good looking as her brother, but she discovers that her talent lies in singing. Includes Spanish
vocabulary. [1. Self-perception—Fiction. 2. Singing—Fiction. 3. Brothers and sisters—Fiction. 4. Toads—Fiction.
5. Animals—Fiction. 6. Stories in rhyme.] I. Garofoli, Viviana, ill. II. Title. PZ8.3.E514Sop 2006 [E]—dc22 2005003536
ISBN 0-399-24199-X 10 9 8 7 6 5 4 3 2 1 First Impression

GLOSSARY

ABEJA (ah BEH hah) bee

ACTRIZ (ahk TREECE) actress

ALEGRÍA (ah leh GREE ah) joy

BOCA (BOE kah) mouth

DÍA (DEE ah) day

FEA (FEH ah) ugly

FELIZ (feh LEECE) happy

FANTÁSTICOS (fahn TAHS tee koce) fantastic

GRUPO (GROO poe) group

GUAPA (GWAH pah) good-looking (feminine)

GUAPO (GWAH poe) good-looking (masculine)

HERMANA (ehr MAH nah) sister

HERMANO (ehr MAH noe) brother

LUNA (LOO nah) moon

MÚSICA (MOO see kah) music

OJOS (OH hoce) eyes

PARTIDOS (pahr TEE doce) games

PEQUEÑO (peh KEH nyoe) little

PESTAÑAS (pehs TAHN yahs) eyelashes

RANAS (RRAH nah) frogs

RÍO (RREE oe) river

SAPO (SAH poe) toad

SUEÑO (SWEH nyoe) dream

TORTUGAS (tohr TOO gahs) turtles

TROFEO (troe FEH oe) trophy

TRONCO (TRONE koe) log

VERRUGAS (veh RROO gahs) warts

VESTIDOS (vehs TEE doce) dresses

VOCES (VOE sehs) voices

VOZ (VOCE) voice

Sophie the toad, the wart-covered **sapo**,
was **fea**—so ugly. Her brother was **guapo**.

His toad warts—**verrugas**—were cuter and smaller.
He was brighter and shinier, thinner and taller.

He had lovely lashes, **pestañas** so curly.
Sophie's were skimpy and short, not too girly.

"I know you're my sister—**hermana**," said Vince.
"But you're not good-looking, and I am a prince!"

Her brother—**hermano**—had dozens of trophies.
They sat on the mantel, not one of them Sophie's!

Trophies for modeling—the best in the bog.
Sophie felt bad and hopped down to her log.

She sat on her **tronco** and sang,
"Why not me?
And why is my brother
as cute as can be?"

Her song voice—her **voz**—
was measured and clear.
She had perfect pitch and a very good ear.

She clutched her small toad—her **sapo pequeño**,
then drifted to sleep and dreamed a good **sueño**.

She dreamed she was pretty with wonderful eyes—
with **ojos fantásticos**. Then a surprise!

"Sophie the model! Come try on this gown.
Come pose for our picture. Keep smiling. Don't frown!"

For hours Sophie tried on their dresses—**vestidos**,
and missed all the fun outdoor games—the **partidos**.

Her mouth—her big **boca**—was too tired to smile.
She was fed up with posing and strutting her style.

"Well, this is no fun!" Then Sophie awoke.

"Me, be a model?

Why, I'd rather croak!"

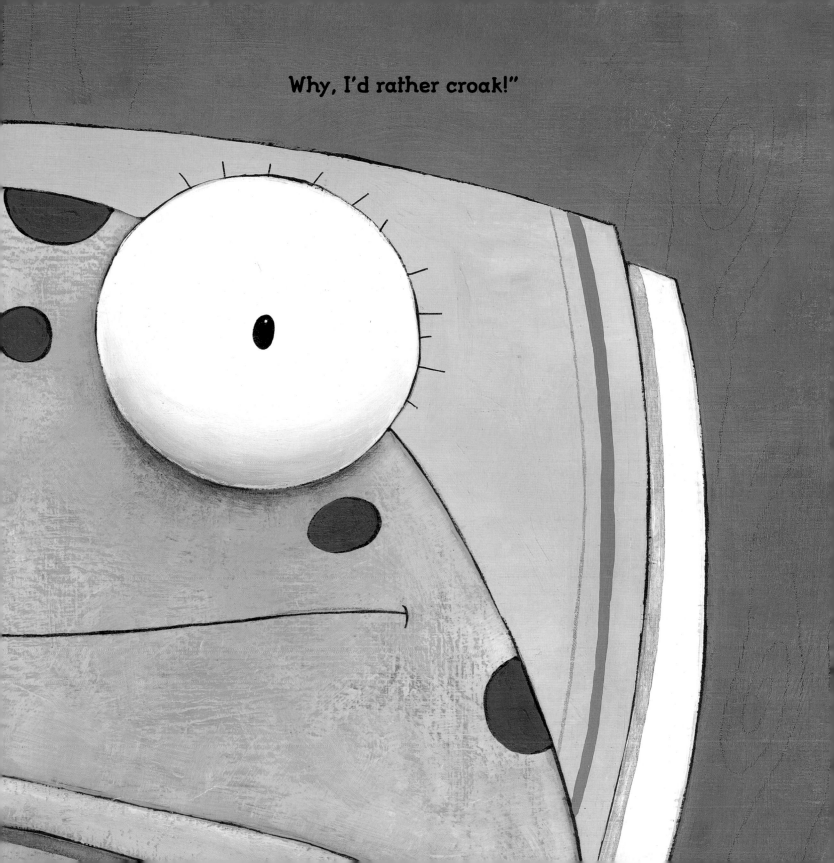

"Then come croak with us,"
said a toad near her log.
"Come sing with our **grupo**.
We meet by the bog."

"Come singing?" said Sophie.
"I do like to croon."
So she joined them that night
by the light of the moon.

The **luna** shone brightly,
so round in the sky,
and Sophie sang loudly,
not one wee bit shy.

The music—the **música**—
sounded so right.
Their voices—toad **voces**—
rang into the night.

The singing made Sophie so happy—**feliz**,
she felt like a beautiful actress—**actriz**.

Then one special day—a very big **día**—
her small homely eyes lit with joy—**alegría**.

You see, the Toadettes had their eyes on a prize,
but some toads were ill since they'd eaten bad flies.

So they asked her to sing
all alone on the stage.
Could she do a solo,
at her tender age?

Her mouth was too big,
and her warts were too bumpy.
She knew she could sing,
but her heart was so jumpy.

"Do I need some spot cream?"
"No, go as you are."
"You'll be great! You look perfect!" they said.
"You're our star!"

The first group went on,
the Hopper Quartet.
Then **ranas**—two frogs—
performed a duet.

Then yodeling turtles—**tortugas**—a trio,
their bald necks stretched out to the river—the **río**.

An **abeja** quintet—the Bee Stingers Five—
were swinging and singing and brought on the jive.

But during her solo,
small Sophie's sweet voice
drove the audience wild,
left the judges no choice.

They gave her the trophy—
trofeo—her first!
And she was so proud,
she thought she would burst.

"My sister, a winner!"
Vince puffed out his chest.
"You're not just a singer.
You're clearly the best."

Back home, on the mantel, he made her a spot.
"The space isn't much, but it's all that I've got."

"No, thanks," Sophie said as she eyed her reflection.
"I'll need much more room for *my* trophy collection."